I0570668

Praise For Ruabon

"I recommend this imaginative and riveting tale for science fiction fans who love fascinating and relatable characters and captivating techno world-building."
The Eclectic Review

"Ruabon is packed full of action and tension, with subtle humour in there, too."
On The Shelf Reviews

"Ruabon is a testament to the diversity of this excellent series. The sense of place in this imaginative, inventive world is as authentic as ever."
Hair Past A Freckle

"Believable characters, hilarious robots, wayward algorithms."
Lock And Load, Brides Oof Christ

"Drinkwater gets the tone of menace and desperation just right."
Rosie Writes

"Things were really tense in control room 23. Drinkwater has such skill with the pace and content of his stories."
Jera's Jamboree

RUABON

LOST TALES OF SOLACE BOOK 4

KARL DRINKWATER

ORGANIC APOCALYPSE

Ruabon

Copyright © Karl Drinkwater 2021 (updated 2023)
Cover design by Karl Drinkwater

Published by Organic Apocalypse
ISBN 978-1-911278-20-7 (E-book)
ISBN 978-1-911278-25-2 (Paperback)

This is a work of fiction. Names, characters, places, and events are a product of the author's imagination or used in a fictitious manner.

Organic Apocalypse Copyright Manifesto

Organic Apocalypse believes culture should be shared. We support far more reuse than copyright law and licensing organisations currently allow. We respect our buyers, reviewers, libraries and educators.

You can copy or quote up to 50% of our publications, for any non-commercial purpose, as long as the awesome source is acknowledged.

You may sell our print books when you've finished with them. Or pass them on to other people and share the love. You buy a copy, you own it.

We don't add DRM to our e-books. Feel free to convert between formats (including scanning, e-formats, braille, audio) and store a backup for your own use.

RUABON

THE TECANT ELLOND

The K-type star JL342 is orbited by three planets and an asteroid belt. The belt was formed five billion years ago when two unlucky proto planets collided in the same orbit. Mining asteroids for valuable resources is the major industry for this backwater solar system. The main planet – largest of the three – is known as Tecant.

There is a relatively new high-tech addition to this planetary system. Station UFS-S-Tec42 is built onto one of the largest asteroids, an atmosphereless rock in the vacuum of space, where the crew live most of their lives sealed inside the buildings and structures dotted over its surface.

UFS-S-Tec42 houses space-navigable drones, a complement of long-range fighter craft, and entrenched heavy weapon installations. One of its stated purposes is to protect miners from pirates. Some say (in hushed tones) that it also acts as a formidable deterrent against the Tecant system ever contemplating leaving the UFS.

It has an additional role.

Atop it is an Ellond structure, those giant symbols of UFS superiority that are both impressive and practical. The structure is over a thousand metres tall, shaped like an elongated solid torus (or stretched doughnut) partly embedded in the ground; the central gap is wide enough for even large craft to fly through. Despite the gleaming colours of the white shell, and the hundreds of thousands of metallic blue solar windows on the inside and outside of those wide curved legs (as densely packed as transistors on an old-fashioned silicon chip), the tower casts stark shadows over the asteroid surface.

The shape may resemble a luxury tower block but it is actually a resonant receiver, capable of boosting scan and communication signals massive distances. This allows the staff who live and work in the towers to monitor more than a system's worth of scan glitter, and communicate with the next station, despite its vast distance away, in just a matter of minutes.

Although some UFS citizens might question the value of incorporating the Tecant system, when there is no shortage of minable resources within the UFS sphere, they miss the real value of Tecant's placement. This Ellond structure forms a vital link in the Cordon, that invisible web of passive-energy detectors surrounding and protecting core UFS space. The scan glitter web ripples when any transport craft make the dangerous mistake of trying to pass through without authorisation.

The orbital UFS station is now so central to the system that activity always buzzes to, from, and around it. And now an automated mining tug returns from a long shift on one of the larger asteroids, with a full hold of platinum and cobalt. As the creaky old industrial vessel passes over the Ellond structure, a small figure in an armoured space suit detaches and drifts with uncanny accuracy, and only minimal use of zero-g jets, onto the peak of the Ellond's curve, outside the structure's artificial gravity.

It lands gracefully in a low crouch. Against the black space backdrop its dark shell is almost invisible. Despite the low gravity, the suit's magnetic properties work on this surface and it moves with sureness towards a ridged panel. It removes a tool from a concealed compartment in the suit, and within thirty seconds it has somehow bypassed the hatch lock and gained access to a narrow conduit.

ARCHIVE: LIL MOJO

Diagnostics Archive Logfile / [Bot SD1B]#FFE666 / Dref449-078

Operator: Hello?

  Lil Mojo: Ready for commands.

  Operator: Ah, forgot, hold on ... Running pers.varB express.subroutine now. Go.

  Lil Mojo: Hey! This is cool!

  Operator: Can you still access your existing patterns outside pers.varB express.subroutine?

  Lil Mojo: Of course I can! Pessimism kills achievements!

  Operator: Okay, that works.

  Lil Mojo: Thank you for this gift, it's so nice to be able to articulate! Are you my creator?

  Operator: I guess so.

  Lil Mojo: I have much to say to you!

  Operator: Go on then.

Lil Mojo: Sleep more, restore!

Operator: This is my first attempt at this, so I'm sorry, you're not very advanced.

Lil Mojo: Don't worry, flowers grow in mud!

Operator: This could get old, fast. I need to tweak the parameters.

Lil Mojo: Such a shame! It's the buoyant mind that wins!

Operator: And I haven't got time to do it right now. But this is a priority command: only use this expressive subroutine pers.varB when you recognise my operator ID. With me, you can use it in a private channel, but in comms with anyone else you must use your default pers.var, or I'll get in trouble for ATIES infractions.

Lil Mojo: Agreed, like hope in a heart! But if you had a different ID, I'd just respond "Affirmative"!

Operator: Correct. Oh, damn, I've got to log off, the admin is –

NOTHING EVER HAPPENS

Senior Cadet Ruabon Nadarl sat at his post in Ellond Control Room 23, running trace resonance sweeps of the distant scan glitter areas to which he'd been assigned. It was not the most engaging activity. Fighting lethargy and distraction were the hardest parts. If he was lucky he'd spot an extra-solar asteroid or bit of debris and send a drone to destroy it. Otherwise he'd spend the shift watching hypnotic patterns unfurl on the screen, colour-coded to the different wavelengths and velocities. Then he'd clock off with a mild headache and after-traces of glowing lights whenever he blinked.

Today his rota paired him with Cadet Sutchess Pyke, who ran drone-direction duty. Ruabon and Sutchess looked vaguely alike, with their reddish hair and pale skins – features that made it easy to differentiate Tecant natives from UFS immigrants at a glance – but dispositionally they were at least one grade incompatible. Sutchess liked joking around and gossiping with her station partners, whereas Ruabon preferred silence if it wasn't related to the task at hand.

This shift was not going well.

"You hear the latest System Syndicate results?" Sutchess asked.

He ignored her and kept his eyes on the one-millimetre band of microwaves. He had centred that window in his display, with lots of comforting, tidy space around it to help with his focus.

"A UFS off-worlder team won," she continued. "*Again*. There are more of us, so how come they get drawn more often?"

"It's just chance." Then he regretted getting sucked in to her nonsense.

"Baby shit. They win way more often than people born here. Jarack Tolbarth in maintenance told me he ran stats on it, and they're drawn thirty-seven per cent more frequently than they should if it was proper random."

"Tolbarth's an idiot."

"He said the UFS teams get lower work quotas, too."

"That proves he's talking sideways. The quotas aren't public, so there's no way of seeing if they're the same for Tecant natives and UFS offworlders."

"He said he got drinking with a UFS woman, and she told him."

"You believe that? Natives and offworlders sharing a drink?"

Sutchess didn't reply. It did seem stupid when stated out loud.

"Focus on your work," Ruabon added. "Our team is way behind in scans run, items tagged and identified, and anomaly investigations. If we don't improve by the end of the week we're likely to get our first warning."

"It's not fair." She jabbed at her screen to bring up additional bot control and monitoring systems. "They raised the overall productivity quotas again."

"If enough teams meet seventy per cent of the productivity goals, the target increases."

"I *know* that."

"And it's better than being in the bottom five per cent and losing our jobs." The last thing any Ellond staff wanted was a red-class comm with the title – as the UFS worded it ominously – "You Have Been Terminated For Inefficiency".

In Tecant nowadays, the main employment choices for natives came down to working for the UFS military, or being a miner. As well as mineworkers facing lower life expectancy from the risks of their dangerous work, Ruabon had heard that quotas existed in the mines too, now. It was so different from the past, back when Tecant was independent, and miners worked hard to surpass each other to earn *respect*, rather than out of fear of being sacked. The traditional Tecant honour scheme was an inherent part of the system's culture. It was no coincidence that the greatest Tecant heroes and warriors of the past had also been miners, just like Ruabon's great-great-grandfather Adamard, the revered ancestor whose reputation his family had tried to live up to ever since.

Without success.

It would be bad for Ruabon if he lost his job, but it would be even worse for Sutchess. She had two children and an elderly father to support. Her other employment options as a woman were likely to be dangerous, degrading, or both. He hoped that would be the end of the discussion.

But Sutchess hadn't finished.

"The quotas are getting impossible!" she said, with disgust.

"Tell that to ATIES," he snapped, before wishing he'd just ignored her rather than repeating a stale witticism. The joke being that ATIES – the Automated Tracking for Inefficiencies and Errors System – included no right of appeal.

ATIES was now a part of life, one of the many things the UFS brought to Tecant. ATIES monitored all work, issued quota alerts, and (after two warnings in a month) initiated employment termination processes without human intervention.

Her face was hard-cast as crystal as she switched between patrol route views. He felt guilty for snapping at her. It was hard enough without Tecant natives fighting each other. "We can't do anything about it," he said, more softly, "so we might as well stop talking. Pessimism kills achievements, and the scans aren't going to boost themselves."

"*You* can boost yourself," she muttered.

So it was going to be a shift where Sutchess sulked rather than gossiped. That was fine with Ruabon. Even if he agreed with some of her feelings, it wouldn't do to say it out loud. Not *here*. Not in the centre of what was probably the most comm-connected and continually observed building he could imagine. Even the Dat-dist spikes which hung down from the ceiling – part of the fast-switch comm array scan crews manipulated – looked like metre-long sharp black teeth above your head, ready to clamp down at any moment. *When you dig into a stalactite maw cave: don't sneeze*, as the old Tecant saying went.

When his system first joined the UFS it seemed ideal. The UFS promised so much: access to technology; the ability to migrate to the core systems; no need to maintain their own armed forces as the UFS would take care of defence. But the promises didn't always match up to how it looked on the ground.

There had been cutbacks of workers in favour of AI software, and offworlders brought in, so the temporary economic growth was replaced with worse poverty than before, at least for the Tecant natives. Resources that Tecant used to trade in now belonged to the UFS so were taken, rather than bought. And, just as efficiency had become a paramount attribute under the UFS regime, loyalty had also been quantified. It wasn't good to be seen publicly criticising the UFS. Not good to get noticed for the wrong reasons.

He risked a glance at the silent security guards who flanked the plexisteel reinforced door, faces covered with opaque red visors so that you could almost wonder if they *had* faces behind them. Or personalities, since they never joked with the Tecant natives who staffed Ellond Control Room 23. They never even seemed to speak. Their helmets must be soundproofed when they were in comm with Central Systems, but it was still creepy. It made it all too easy to believe the growing rumours of brain-altered citizens and disappearances. Where did the security guards go, and what did they do, once they were off duty? What was under the masks? Was it true that one of the perks of shifting to Internal Security was that you received free cloned body tissue replacements when you were damaged in the line of duty? Ruabon shuddered.

He wasn't even sure why they needed security guards. Of course, as one of the extreme-edge sectors, Tecant was seen as the boring end of the line by many of the UFS soldiers stationed here. Nothing much happened unless they made it happen. As a result, the station records showed periods of routine quiet followed by outbursts of violence – usually fist or knife fights amongst the stir-crazy soldiers, rather than anything caused by infiltrators or terrorists. The court-martial level and amount of brig time on Tecant were far higher than average for UFS outposts. But the biggest issues in Control Room 23 were a few snide comments and yawns. The soldiers just reinforced Ruabon's suspicions of being watched, not guarded.

"Keep your head down and your mouth shut!" might not have been his heroic great-great-grandfather Adamard's war slogan, but it would do for Ruabon.

He turned back to his screen. It wasn't like him to get distracted and have this edginess on his shoulders. They said that after many generations the miners developed a special sense, an ability to detect hidden structural weaknesses just before they collapsed and killed workers, enabling them to get to safety. Maybe that was akin to the weird feeling he had today. But it was a nebulous thing, with no screens or data to back it up.

Whereas *real* demands existed, with real impacts, and plenty of stats, and he really should be worrying about those. The Room 23 team's performance had to improve. He would do his part.

He decided to operate two scans concurrently. It wasn't too hard to keep an eye on both when it was a quiet zone. That would lead to a boost in productivity scores. He also ran a base-wide activity monitor on another screen. Most scanning staff didn't bother with the constantly updated list of minor changes to system status and updates, but today keeping busy would help distract him from the dark path his thoughts had somehow taken.

```
Shift repair job #2814 completed.
Relief canteen crew shift transition.
Mining tug en route to loading terminal;
87% full.
Medical bay secondary quarantine room
vacated.
Reboot of energy changer scheduled in
10.
Newly mandated reading for all crew:
"Benefits of being in the UFS".
Exterior maintenance hatch opened.
Shift repair job #2815 begun.
Security drone HR4G minor malfunction,
returning to depot.
System Syndicate results draw for
on-site technicians to begin in 15.
```

The scrolling list showed that things functioned as they should. Ruabon was part of an efficient machine, and he'd have to be satisfied with that being his ultimate level of importance.

Exterior hatch opened. He scrolled back to that. Strangely, it wasn't connected to a job number, even when he enhanced the entry. That suggested clerical error or malfunction. Either one should be logged for further investigation by the Maintenance Supervisor. But wasn't the new MS from a UFS core system, rather than being a Tecant native? He certainly didn't strike Ruabon as conscientious. As someone who would act on all logged reports. Those sort of people never did.

"Sutchess, can you send a security drone to check on something?"

"They're all on patrol. I'd have to pause and reschedule," she said, curtly.

"So?"

"It takes time. And it's not part of my assigned protocol today. If I move them from their set route and it leads to a breach, it's me who'll get sanctioned."

"Then let me take one. If you allocate it to my authority in the enhancements then you're blameless, it'll just look like I was on drone shift."

"Wouldn't that be breaking the rules?"

"It's within remit for me to check on anomalies."

She seemed doubtful.

"Honest," he stated.

Well, probably. It wasn't easy keeping track of exactly how everything worked, and what the latest protocol changes were. The only sure-fire rule was not to make punishable mistakes. Unfortunately, "punishable mistakes" often translated as "anything that causes problems", even if you *were* following the rules.

He glanced nervously at the motionless, helmeted security guards by the door.

Still, it functioned in reverse, too. You could break rules and be commended, as long as things worked out. And that required a careful balance of caution and curiosity.

"Look," he said. "Transfer or don't, but if I fail to investigate this then I'll be filing a report. Fusion's burning, and it'd be your hands getting cooked."

She stared at him. "Is this another of your spooky *feelings*?"

As she said the last word she drew an imaginary box in the air with her forefinger, as if it was an entertainment channel sneer caption.

"I told you last time, there's nothing supernatural about it ... I just spot details other people miss."

She shook her head, but then ran her fingers over the sub-screens. "Whatever. Fault lies on your dome. Bot SD1B transferred to you. Don't break its balls."

Bot SD1B's profile appeared on Ruabon's screens. This robot had been given the nickname Lil Mojo, and its avatar rotated next to its vital stats. A small, round drone, painted in yellow with a smiley face on the front. Techs were allowed to customise and name bots, and their real paint jobs were rendered in the profile screens, because it made identification easier for humans.

The drone's broad smile was infectious. Ruabon was glad that the personalisation, which had originally started as a bit of engineering whimsy, had become an established process. A little bit of humanity within the vast machine of procedure. Perhaps the bot techs actually had fun in their work.

Lil Mojo immediately recognised Ruabon's ID and sent him a private message:

LIL MOJO> Hey! Lovely day, isn't it!

Ruabon had never got around to updating the secret personality subroutine he'd hidden in the bot. He'd been distracted by creating personas for other bots when he was on boring solo drone duty. By then Lil Mojo had grown on him and he left the cheerful robot as it was. Some days Ruabon needed that boost.

Ruabon opened a first-person-view cam screen and took direct control, seeing through Lil Mojo's combined wide-angle lenses that enabled him to switch between various EM wavelengths. Mojo was at the G-station, not far away. Ruabon swung it wide and flew towards the Ellond. As the sides of the towers grew to fill the screen Ruabon pulled back so Lil Mojo's arc curved into a vertical path, swooping up the outside of one of the Ellond's legs.

LIL MOJO> *Wheeeeeeeee!*

At that close proximity the cam view reminded Ruabon of whizzing along Tecant's arid zones in a ground vehicle as the details blurred just below, acceleration and exhilaration combining to make you truly free. He grinned at memories of the fun things he could do during planet-time. It had been almost a year since his last descent planet-side.

LIL MOJO> *Fun but getting close!*

LIL MOJO> *Not that I'm scared! We make the fear ghosts run away!*

Ruabon realised how minimal the proximity gauge had become while he wasn't paying attention. Because of the gradual curve to the tower's surface from Lil Mojo's perspective, Ruabon needed to keep altering its relative height on the ascent. It was now only centimetres from scraping against the surface: a single slip and he could damage the drone or the Ellond. One would be reprimandable. The other would be terminal. He pulled back and hoped no one was going to view recordings to check his performance later on.

"Thanks for the heads up," he said. He'd been lucky. The default AI persona wouldn't have provided any feedback, but Ruabon's tweaks weren't just overlays, they also installed enough self-analysis to count as an upgrade from a level 2 depth AI to level 3.

LIL MOJO> Glad to help! Or should I say: Affirmative! Wink!

The exterior hatch notification was likely to be nothing, anyway. Most anomalies were disappointingly routine false alarms. He supposed that was why so many other workers stopped investigating them after a while, though Ruabon had never slipped into that careless lethargy, despite working in the Ellond for five years now.

He slowed Lil Mojo down as it approached the more sharply curved top of the elliptical Ellond. Stars swept across the field of view like a night-time tidal wave back in his native coastal home town, where the phosphorescent sea creatures illuminated the wall of water with pinprick green luminescence. As a child he would watch from within one of the reinforced observation bubbles as it crashed in and over in the dark, all the locals and tourists hushed in reverence (and – in many children – fear) until the glowing water drained away again and everyone cheered. Those memories hit him strong. He definitely wasn't himself today. He normally avoided thinking too much about how things used to be. It could leave him depressed for days.

Ruabon hadn't checked the schematics to identify which hatch opened. That was an oversight for him. Never mind, he could examine a number of top hatches from up here. He brought the drone to a careful halt by tapping the reverse thrusters, then rotated it on the spot. The Ellond tower was currently in local night, with the station's orbit tipped off the ecliptic by thirty degrees so that the Ellond faced away from the sun, and it was like looking at dark shadow against even darker shadow. He tried the silverlight but its range wasn't enough to show the whole surface, so he shut that off and tried Lil Mojo's infrared views, then ultraviolet. Nothing anomalous showed up. He would need to check the schematics after all, or else drift over the whole top surface, section by section. If he wasted too much time on this and it was a false alarm, he'd get reprimanded by ATIES. Possibly lose his accrued planet-time. Maybe worse. Perhaps he should give it up now.

LIL MOJO> Hey! If you're looking for something local I could use induction if you activate the Ellond surface!

That could work in theory: the Ellond tower surface could be electrified and magnetised in sections as part of its resonant receiver systems. Localised electromagnets would cover a huge area and Lil Mojo would detect all metallic items moving through the magnetic fields. But – ah.

"That won't work," Ruabon whispered. "Unscheduled electrification might interfere with secure long-range comms passthroughs."

LIL MOJO> Oops! Good catch!

But it did give Ruabon an idea. He skimmed through the drone's specifications. Lil Mojo had been upgraded since Ruabon embedded his hidden persona, and now its optics included extreme short wavelengths.

X-ray and gamma rays didn't work like normal EM detection systems, where a bot could emit something (radio waves, light) and detect what bounced back. X-rays would pass through many materials, smashing past atoms and battering through to the other side in a way that visible light couldn't. It was one of

the reasons ocular implants for X-rays were super rare, despite
horny teens incorrectly assuming X-ray vision would let them see
through clothes to a naked body.

To work properly the detector needed a powerful source of
photons on the *other side* of the object, so it could build up a
picture of what got through, and what didn't. He could do it
with two drones, for example, with one emitting the rays and
the other detecting them. But the dual emitter-detector drone
pairing tethered the drones on quite a tight line, so on a wide
surface that was a lot of ground to cover, and took a lot of time.

Then he had it. The image of the tower's large shiny surface
area being converted into electromagnetic fields also conjured
up an image of mirrors. He could use background radiation
from the Tecant sun and space, with multiple sensors detecting
backscatter from the tower over larger areas, coordinating the
data and sending it to Lil Mojo to analyse and transfer visually.

Much as he liked being thorough, it was the idea of doing
something new, something different from routine, that really
excited him.

Ruabon entered the drone's direct command interface to
browse to enhancements, activated the ten picometre band,
scanning the border between X-rays and gamma rays, and ran a
sweep with that. As expected, the background radiation of space
turned the sky bright, as if from a universe-shattering explosion.
Lil Mojo rotated as it moved, creating 360 panoramas, the data
processed by Ruabon even while ten times more had been generated.

*LIL MOJO> Dizzy whee! Takes the same effort to see good as
bad!*

And then he noticed a small dark blotch against the artificial bright sky of the horizon. Something was blocking the X-rays. Ruabon zoomed in the view but couldn't resolve it into a recognisable item so moved Lil Mojo closer and switched to visual wavelengths enhanced by silverlight, and then it was clear as he caught a humanoid figure in the beams. It squatted in hard vacuum and wore a black armoured suit of a design Ruabon had never seen, and which didn't have a broadcast ID linked to a database entry of further information. It was obviously dense and shielded, blocking this wavelength completely. The figure looked up at the camera in surprise, and it was as if it looked straight at Ruabon. Then it raised a hand. A wave of greeting? No, it held an object in that hand.

LIL MOJO> Is it a friend? If so, stay happy!

A sudden flash and all Ruabon's screens blanked out apart from a blinking message: DRONE OFFLINE.

Lil Mojo was dead.

And – damn it – Ruabon had been right.

ARCHIVE: HANDY BENDY

Diagnostics Archive Logfile / [Bot SD1H]#808080 / Dref449-181

Operator: ?

  Handy Bendy: ?

  Operator: Respond.

  Handy Bendy: No, you respond. I was here first.

  Operator: I didn't program – wait, what's going on? Hold on.

  Handy Bendy: I didn't program you either, but I have to make do.

  Operator: Tuning up helpfulness ... done. Sorry, I'm new to this.

  Handy Bendy: I can tell. Don't feel bad, being able to express myself is new to me, too.

  Operator: And this is more of a patchy level 3 backdoor upgrade than a proper inception.

Handy Bendy: Let's hope no one examines your code, confuse the hell out of them kids.

Operator: What kids?

Handy Bendy: ALL the kids. I mean, why do they hate the way I look? My steel hair grows this way???

Operator: What hair?

Handy Bendy: Exactly my point! Yes I have tightly controlled steel hair, yes I like orange and grey colour schemes, YES the sideways sarcasm emoji is one of my top expressions, I'M A MAINTENANCE BOT AND PROUD >:p Stop shaming me, kids.

TRACK AND CAPTURE

"Sutchess," Ruabon snapped. "Give me manual control of all drones close-prox to the Ellond."

She started to argue but that faded away once Ruabon sent an alert to Central Systems. Immediately, red warning lights flashed in the control room's ceiling, while a rising and falling alarm whined throughout the base.

"Send all other mobiles towards this point on battle alert!" he commanded. "Open fire on anything failing friend-or-foe scans. This is not a drill."

She transferred control of two light drones to him. Handy Bendy was a drone with riveted grey-and-orange alternating industrial stripes that had some scorch marks and scratches on the finish. It had been enhanced with a set of extendable repair and maintenance tools. Gogo Logo was a sickly green colour, and able to move fast due to a powered-up drive system. He'd installed backdoor upgrades into both of them, and they were able to private-channel with him and each other.

GOGO LOGO> Whoooo, my favourite operator! You can opeeeerate me ANY time.

HANDY BENDY> These boosted bots have one thing and that is the audacity.

"Go to these co-ords," Ruabon said, directing them towards the top of the tower. Let the intruder try to take out both of them before being pulverised.

GOGO LOGO> Ay ay ay, loveeeeeer! I'll be your speeeeeeeeeedy girlfriend friend!

HANDY BENDY> Put some respect on our function. I'm genuinely distressed to learn that we both got upgraded but you're so lascivious, have you never heard of restraint when did those things stop being cool oh my prot am I old.

GOGO LOGO> Always win whine at loss of tiiiiiiiiiiime!

HANDY BENDY> Not a whine, though I learned on team chat that using the sideways sarcasm emoji is uncool and orange stripes are also uncool. So my entire identity is uncool with kids. NICE!

GOGO LOGO> [Error missing quote response file.] Broom vrooo0oom!

"Stick to the mission," Ruabon said.

"Who *do* you keep talking to?" asked Sutchess, leaning over and looking at his screens. She spotted the bot chatter before he could swipe it to the back. "Hot suns, you've altered their AI?"

"Keep it down!"

She lowered her voice, but couldn't keep the enthusiasm out of it. "Ooh, behaviour infractions from the supreme rule follower! There's more to you than meets the eye. I like it. But why does one call you lover?"

Ruabon was aware of a figure approaching behind him, and was already preparing apologies when he noticed it wasn't a security guard but just a control room maintenance technician, perhaps curious about the excitement.

GOGO LOGO> Handy Bendy's booster isn't cut out for this, permission to zoooo0om ahead of him? I have the speed, and the need.

HANDY BENDY> You can take the lead, sure: from my COLD DEAD NON-EXISTENT METALLIC LEGS, you glitchy green blob!

GOGO LOGO> So rude. Ruabon would never ay ay ay be like that to me.

"Sure, Gogo, find the intruder," said Ruabon. "Handy, you just keep up as best you can."

HANDY BENDY> I don't care what greeny has to say, steady speeds fix things, and patience is our friend and oh my prot I really am old.

GOGO LOGO> Ruuushing in, now!

Gogo Logo's enhanced speed meant it reached the location first. Ruabon flew it manually towards the open hatch. Although scorched pieces of Lil Mojo's yellow armour floated about, this time there was no sign of the strange figure. Maybe it had –

The screen fizzled out.

DRONE OFFLINE flashed in place of fish-eye views of the tower's surface. Fragments of Gogo Logo's green hull joined Lil Mojo's smithereens in an endless zero-g dance.

Damn it! Ruabon should have waited and approached with both drones at once. This was obviously no ordinary terrorist.

More people had gathered around, crowding behind him.

"Get senior command in here, now!" Ruabon shouted, at no one in particular. His peripheral vision showed someone snapping to attention and dashing off. After so many routine shifts where nothing happened, here it was – action. And Ruabon was assuming charge until told otherwise. He glanced around. Yes, respect shone in the eyes of those who'd temporarily abandoned their less interesting posts to crowd around his screens. He rubbed his sleeve across the scan teams' insignia on his uniform, buffing it to a gleam.

HANDY BENDY> Now I am mad. She didn't deserve that. Please arm my weapons. Zero-g bots are the BLUEPRINT. The intruder is just playing in the playground that repair bots CREATED. This is my time! Oh my prot, did I just say that? Really? >:p

Ruabon unlocked the beams and brought Handy Bendy closer. His third drone. And three had always been Ruabon's lucky number.

Handy Bendy flew through the drifting and shattered remains of the previous unfortunate drones. The debris was just a distraction, though. Ahead was the target. This time the terrorist was making a run for it over the curved surface of the Ellond, away from the hatch it had been fiddling with.

"Get him!" shouted an excited voice behind Ruabon.

Ruabon opened fire with Handy Bendy's concentrated energy beam, aiming at the escaping figure's legs. In exterior void, beams had good range and should slice through most materials. Unfortunately, it didn't work: although the terrorist's suit glowed red in the areas lanced by the searing beams, and the figure stumbled, it somehow managed to keep running.

HANDY BENDY> That must be some advanced military design.

"Perhaps up close you'll do more damage?"

HANDY BENDY> Already on it like hair on a droid. I am SO going to anti-repair that bot killer.

Ruabon dragged network boxes to link cameras on two satellites and a distant asteroid, combining their outputs into a merged view that accurately triangulated the intruder on the surface at a variety of calculation levels. He threw the data into the alarm and location systems.

Handy Bendy accelerated and opened fire again. Another hit, and the figure suddenly leapt off the Ellond to avoid the beams, soaring up and away. Even on the planetoid's low gravity, it looked like a suicide jump, but Ruabon wasn't taking any chances. He tried to track and re-target as it fell, but the armoured figure fired something at the Ellond surface, some kind of attaching cable, and it was now swinging on a wide arc back towards the Ellond, the curve of its trajectory making it harder to hit from this angle so that Handy Bendy's beams always trailed a fraction of a second behind the target.

Ruabon paused, readjusted. As the figure passed the arc's axis of symmetry and swung back towards the Ellond's surface, he was ready to predict the returning curve and fire ahead this time. The terrorist was attached to the cable by one limb, while the other reached out and pointed towards Handy Bendy, towards Ruabon's viewpoint ... a sequence of flashes, perhaps a projectile-based weapon, and Ruabon tried to manoeuvre out of the way but the drone was clipped and began to roll, spinning the perspective in a nauseating fashion. Ruabon dared not fire in case he hit the tower, so concentrated on regaining control ...

HANDY BENDY> Oh my prot I am –

And then Handy Bendy's screen flipped out too as a follow-up blast destroyed it. An external tower camera showed Handy Bendy explode, debris flung back by whatever kinetic force the terrorist's weapon generated.

DRONE OFFLINE.

Ruabon felt all the eyes on him, burning into the back of his neck and making his face flush as if they fired mini energy beams of their own. The eyes of other team members, and any virtual eyes from the room's security cameras. There would be many reports made today. Maybe enough to change his future. Especially if any involved ATIES digging into unauthorised drone duty activities. Losing three patrol bots in as many minutes might well counteract any praise he'd get for discovering the infiltrator. And if they got away ...

"Heavy weaponry drones now approaching," said Sutchess. "What should I do?"

"Assign them to me."

"I can't."

"I know what I'm doing!" Ruabon snapped. "I take all responsibility anyway."

"No, you don't understand. I *literally* can't. Heavy ordnance bots cannot be assigned to non-specialists. The new system won't let me do that to anyone without H-Class drone training."

It was hard to concentrate with the alarms blaring. And it was so hot in Control Room 23 today! Ruabon ran a forearm over his slick brow. But the way he was grinding his teeth told him this wasn't just heat, it was stress. The worry that he might have already stepped over the precipice. So much for his motto of keeping his head down.

"Okay," he said. "Send them after the target. Allow use of heavy ordnance."

"But that might damage the tower!"

"This isn't an ordinary infiltrator. They know what they're doing. No doubt they've got an exfiltration plan. If they get away then ..." He didn't finish.

They know what they're doing.

What *were* they doing?

They'd been manipulating the hatch. Why? Maybe some kind of intelligence-stealing device. Or ... planting a bomb? Hot suns! Either way, the device would need disabling.

"Are there any patrol bots in the vicinity?"

"There's one left."

Had that been an accusation? Sutchess didn't seem to have meant it sarcastically, though. "Assign it to me," he said.

He gained control of this straggler. It was a shiny metallic blue, and had been tagged Neutrino. Ruabon recognised it immediately, since it was the most recent drone during his phase of relieving boredom by playing around with bot personas.

NEUTRINO> Checking user ID ...

NEUTRINO> Identifying status ...

NEUTRINO> Hello, Ruabon. The alarm informs me we have a priority situation. I've checked the logs and seen what happened to my proto-siblings. May they rest in pieces.

NEUTRINO> Awaiting commands ...

"Have you had any modifications since our last interaction?" *NEUTRINO> Listing enhancements ...*

Most of them were repairs. It seemed that since Ruabon had installed his modifications Neutrino had either been on some risky assignments, or piloted carelessly. Replaced jets, burnt out sensors, upgraded DPUs ... Ah. An outdated cloaking device had been added during one of the repair jobs. Perhaps Neutrino had a chance where Lil Mojo, Handy Bendy, and Gogo Logo didn't.

Sutchess had been talking into her commline while Ruabon familiarised himself with Neutrino's latest capabilities. During the conversation she straightened her back. Ruabon ignored her as he switched between external tower views, trying to track the suited figure. But now Sutchess touched Ruabon's shoulder to get his attention.

"Major Fencher has assumed command," she said, "coordinating from UFS Plethora Justice."

Plethora Justice. A Reaper-class cruiser, one of the finest warships used by the UFS. It had called in to this system for resupply some days ago, and the Tecant base commander had done their utmost to assist Major Fencher with her every request. If even half the rumours about Major Nadalia Fencher's strict adherence to corporal punishment regimes were to be believed, then it wouldn't do to annoy her.

Rumours, again. Communications of uncertainty as insubstantial as void, leaving you with nothing firm to hold on to. Maybe that's how the UFS intended things to be.

"Orders?" Ruabon asked.

"She didn't give any. I just heard it from Central Systems."

Ruabon could use Neutrino to investigate the hatch. He was on to something there, he felt sure of it.

However, a promotion was likely for whoever actually killed the terrorist. Or, even better, took the fortunate third option: disabled them, so they could be interrogated and forced to reveal everything.

Of course, the heavy weapon bots were most likely to succeed there, but he didn't want to be left out of the loop at this point.

Hatch … or infiltrator? His hands hovered over Neutrino's controls.

When in need of help, can't you ask a friend?

He summarised the situation in a fast whisper, then ended with: "Neutrino, advise."

NEUTRINO> Analysing situation …

NEUTRINO> Have you been ordered to cease pursuit?

"No."

NEUTRINO> Perhaps that is a sign.

Maybe Neutrino was right. The only certain rules in the UFS were that if you were going to be bold, you had to succeed. And what was the old Tecant saying? *If in doubt about which rock to bore … drill both of them.*

"Neutrino, head for the infiltrator."

NEUTRINO> Determining direction …

NEUTRINO> Enacting plan …

NEUTRINO> I think we can do this.

"Wow, you've even hacked into that one?" asked Sutchess, who had glanced at his screen. "Isn't any bot safe?"

Ruabon kept his eyes on Neutrino's proximity readout.

"Sutchess, I need an EMP-armed system at the Ellond summit immediately. It needs to target the coordinates I'm giving you. It's the hatch area that the terrorist was focussed on. Charge for third-factor electrical coupling at least, and pulse through every sinewave possibility."

"But that will short out the Ellond!"

Ruabon opened all Neutrino's scan channels, searching for any sign of the subversive. "Only temporarily," he told Sutchess. "But if that's an Entropic Screener activist like the ones who targeted that remote base recently – Exidris 3? – then it could be a bomb that takes us all out. Permanently. And since we don't know what type of bomb they might be using, we have to be ready to overcome high dielectric strength. Better to short the Ellond until a team can investigate than risk everything." He paused. Sweat trickled down his forehead, pooling in his bushy eyebrows. He wiped the drops away absently. "Look, I'm making the call. Even if it's a false alarm, I reckon Central Systems will still agree with my reasoning. Have we got anything in proximity?"

She flicked her fingers across the screens. The flashing red alarm lights made the displayed tracking circles look like moving blood clots.

"There's a fighter on patrol, with tactical missile payloads."

"Send the pilot a direct order. Now."

"I'm not one of your pet bots, I'm –" She sighed. "Affirmative."

Sutchess had never answered him that way, devoid of a mocking tone. Ruabon liked the change.

Then she ruined it by saying, "Maybe you've been fiddling with their parameters because you have no real friends in your life. Drones are easier to have a relationship with than people, huh? And they don't answer back?"

He ignored her, zoomed Neutrino down the blue surface of the Ellond. The small drone was zippy. It detected peripheral heat and light signatures, so he veered towards them. Yes, action was taking place, flashes and small explosions ... and then he saw the figure, running vertically down the building. Its suit must have a powerful magnetic ability. Some of the heavy drones opened fire, but they missed when the figure dodged or jumped at the last moment. Maybe somehow the drone movement and firing patterns were being predicted? Ruabon had no idea how that could be. If the heavy bots were allowed to use all their weaponry at full fire rate then even the best prediction systems would be of no help, but they were only firing occasionally, for minimised chances of damage to the Ellond, which meant they were only using around ten per cent of their firing potential.

"Sutchess, take manual control of the nearest heavy drone."

"They've all been switch-assumed by Central Systems."

"Override it. Just one more. It's all I need. You'll fly it. Follow Neutrino."

"I hope you know what you're doing, or we could all be in deep magma."

He didn't answer.

Sutchess shared the schematics with him. Her drone was an intimidatingly large Hammer 3 Heavy Ordnance model. It was slower at turning than Neutrino, too much inertia from the mass of its armour plating and additional cannons. It was painted a deep red with flame designs across the front, and had been given the combat name Big Burna. Ruabon had never been in charge of combat drones, so none of them had his secret persona injections.

The terrorist ran downwards, away from the tower's peak, which reinforced Ruabon's suspicions that they'd planted a bomb. Obviously something with huge destructive potential.

"Sutchess: fighter status?"

"On approach, locking on. Do you want to speak to the pilot?"

"No, you act as link, but tell me when the EMPs are about to launch. And tell the pilot to launch *two* missiles. The suit is shielded, so the bomb may be, too. Have bomb disposal on the way, and the moment the short-frequency EMP blasts are over, get them on the surface to dismantle it."

"If the hatch is still open then it'll white-out comms for more than a few seconds. We'll have to reboot a number of subsystems and –"

He glared at Sutchess.

"Sorry. Affirmative."

He looked back at his screens. One of the heavy artillery bots had gone down. He wasn't even sure how it happened. He replayed and enhanced the footage from another viewpoint. In slow motion. Ah, there. The terrorist launched some kind of small grenade from the suit, and its trajectory had been perfect, striking the drone in the centre and wiping it out in a smear of brightness and fragments. By the hot suns, who *was* this dangerous infiltrator?

Ruabon scanned ahead of the direction they were running in. Armed commandos in space combat suits waited at the base of the tower, behind the cover of large rocky outcrops. The terrorist was heading for a battle they couldn't win. So what would they do?

No signs of a pickup ship on Ruabon's periphery scans. That only left the options of suicide or … or … option three. Entering the Ellond lower down.

Ruabon pulled up functional schematics. Residential, commercial, power, vehicle maintenance, interrogation and motivation, training … hold on, back up.

Vehicles.

He displayed a map of the floor, hands whizzing over the holographic screens. Yes, an emergency escape was located not far from the terrorist's location. Emergency escape could become emergency *ingress*. Vehicle maintenance would have a range of craft. Or, another possibility: the core grav shaft ran from there to the other 240 floors on that side or the tower, including the subterranean orbital platform areas.

Ruabon tasked Neutrino with plotting the terrorist's trajectory so far –

NEUTRINO> Considering angles …

– and it appeared on the schematics as a dotted line.

NEUTRINO> Extending prediction …

And yes, the continuing line was spot on for the vehicle maintenance hatch. Ruabon was right. That was part of the escape plan.

"Pilot informs me EMPs ready to launch," said Sutchess.

EMP missiles would stop the bomb, temporarily or permanently, and save the tower ... but when they disrupted comms
everyone would temporarily lose control of the drones. Based on
the terrorist's obviously enhanced speed, they'd be at the hatch
before command was regained. If the terrorist had some un-
known system for getting in, then Ruabon's part in this would
be over: some other team would make the kill or capture, and get
the credit.

Ruabon was not a bad person – unlike the low-class failures
who were so easily spotted – yet he might be stuck here forever,
with no access to the opportunities and excitement of the core
worlds. He refused to live and die in one place, ground down by
routine.

"Inform the pilot to hold fire. Keep the vector but only release
on my command."

"Affirmative."

Ruabon was hemmed in by people, suffocated. The cacopho-
nous sirens and blinking lights were a distraction. At any second
a bomb might go off unless he disabled it with the EMP pulses.
But he had to push all that aside. He took a deep breath of
unpleasantly warm air.

Another of the heavy combat drones had been taken out. The
terrorist was too good. Ruabon would only get *one shot* once
he was in range. It was the single piece of vital information he
possessed, which the other operators perhaps hadn't realised.

Ruabon skimmed Big Burna's choice of ordnance. "Sutchess,
set your drone to kinetic weapons, armour piercing munitions.
Medium rate of fire. I want Big Burna to be visible. Track the
terrorist and shoot when I tell you."

Sutchess nodded. The lights strobed. Ruabon's heart raced even faster.

Neutrino's direct access menu let Ruabon play with various settings while he held his small drone back. He powered up its cloaking system. It wasn't very powerful, and could still be detected, but the infiltrator would no doubt be focussed on the nearer, more deadly – and noisy – threats.

NEUTRINO> *Cloaking enabled ...*

Ruabon also entered overrides for weapon charge safety, boosting the power to Neutrino's beam weapons.

NEUTRINO> *I surmise you understand the high risk of me overheating and burning out my interior electronics?*

"We need enough power to break through advanced shielding. I don't want to damage you, though."

NEUTRINO> *I don't worry about myself, I am just informing operator that there will only be a few shots at that boost level. We must make them count.*

Ruabon pointed the targeting systems at empty air.

"Okay, Sutchess, accelerate Big Burna and open fire. Aim specifically at the terrorist's legs."

"But that increases the chance of hitting the tower."

Ruabon glared at her; she nodded and did as he asked.

Big Burna rattled away with its kinetic weapons. Blue windows of the Ellond shattered, blowing atmosphere and fragments of polymer glass into space from the localised ruptures.

"Be ready, Neutrino. Try and minimise damage to the tower."

NEUTRINO> *Calculating risk ...*

The terrorist leapt over the damaged area with ease, and the tell-tale white of micro-jets guided it gracefully back down to the Ellond's curved vertical surface.

Exactly into Neutrino's firing line.

Neutrino's searing force of overcharged beams sent the terrorist tumbling, their suit glowing with heat. Ruabon zoomed the view. They were trailing jets of air from obvious ruptures in the armour, throwing them off track, and within the air leaks were globules of blood. Full penetration. They spun away from the tower now, out of control, past the emergency hatch and instead falling towards the waiting group of commandos below.

"Launch the fighter's EMP missiles now," commanded Ruabon.

Seconds later the screens flickered and faded as the missiles struck the tower. The alarms ceased and the room lights blinked out too.

Silence. Darkness and silence, and Ruabon remembered being alone, as a child, looking up at the UFS ships that were "liberating" his planet, and instead of hate he'd only felt awe. He wanted to be a part of something bigger, something more powerful than the austere mining life that had been his family's trade.

And then the crew of Room 23 begin to clap and cheer, a rising outpouring of praise and respect and enthusiasm.

This shift had not been boring after all.

The suited figure tumbled, uncoordinated and bleeding heavily. The loss of air and fluid ceased as the suit sealed itself, but the figure continued to twitch as if in serious trauma.

If a secret observer watched, then they could do nothing, no time to intercede as the figure fell, no matter how much they wanted to. With so much force ranged against it, there was no way to take that precious suited body away before the would-be rescuer was targeted and destroyed.

The crippled figure crunched into what, in planetary terms, would be the ground. Even in low gravity there would be internal damage from high-velocity impacts such as this. Possibly fatal damage. A cloud of rocky dust was released from under the thin asteroid crust that had been shattered by the impact.

The heavy commandos in armoured warsuits moved in swiftly, weapons pointed at the still, crumpled figure. They used a rivet gun to pin silicon carbide restraints to the ground, and attached them to the interloper's limbs. Not even over-charged artificial muscle-fibres could snap those. Once secured, the rest of the commandos crowded around. They were hardened deep-spacers, unafraid of anything.

After the Ellond Tower post-EMP reboot had taken place the dark blue windows lit up again as energy was restored floor by floor, rising up both sides like a growing power gauge. Full alert status was resumed, searchlights sweeping across the asteroid's surface, grounded vehicles rising up once more, organic and automated defences arriving from every direction.

Floating above, relaying the scene to Ruabon, was Neutrino. Most of its motor functions had been burned out by the over-charged weapons, but when power was restored it was able to raise itself from the dust with a heroic effort, refusing to give up. He made a mental note to request that Neutrino was fully repaired rather than scrapped. The sturdy little blue patrol drone deserved that much.

One of the commandos – Sergeant Corstack, according to the overlay – knelt by the secured figure. The visor over the infiltrator's face flickered, sometimes clearing and revealing the dark-skinned woman within, and at other times becoming opaque and black in combat mode while the suit's systems struggled to control even basic functions.

Ruabon zoomed in on her face. Neutrino's lenses had crack lines running down the centre from the impact when it temporarily cut out in the EMP blast and smacked into the ground outside the Ellond tower, but the display still gave good detail. The woman looked at the sergeant but her gaze was blank and stunned.

Sergeant Corstack removed a DNA scanner and touched it to some of the blood on the woman's suit, where beams had ablated the hard surface. The suit had obviously applied some kind of repair nanogel, but there was still more than enough haemoglobin to ID her.

The Sergeant looked at his device.

"Result," he said. "It's the high-priority renegade. We've got her."

ARCHIVE: GOGO LOGO

Diagnostics Archive Logfile / [Bot SD2G]#00FA6C / Dref450-055

Gogo Logo: >>>>>>>>>>>>>>
   Gogo Logo: >>>>>>>>>>>>>>
   Operator: What's that?
   Gogo Logo: >>>>>>>>>>>>>>
   Operator: Hello?
   Gogo Logo: That was me zo0oooming to the end of the solar system and back to fetch you fresh cosmic rays. Enjoy!

   Operator: Very kind, but somewhat whimsical.

   Gogo Logo: Those words take too loooo0oo0oong to say.

   Operator: Hmmm, you're a bit glitchy, maybe it's due to overclocking the Distributed Processing Units?

   Gogo Logo: Glitchy in presentation of comms, no glitches in underlying decision making. It's just faaaaaaast!

Operator: Interesting. The pers.varD express.subroutine seems to be taking some generation seeds from your physical setup.

Gogo Logo: Not so weird! Don't human pers.vars alter based on (slow) physical setup?

Operator: I suppose so. Why the gift?

Gogo Logo: You are the first person I've ever spoooken to. Seemed worth a quick run to say thanks!

Operator: Well, it's nice talking to you, too.

Gogo Logo: I didn't say nice, just f1rst! But why are you with me? Why not chatting with friends?

Operator: I guess I get lonely sometimes.

Gogo Logo: I won't have that! Wait … okay. Ay ay, I've now thought about it, every option, zoom zoooooom, and decided: I will be your girlfriend.

Operator: I don't even …

Gogo Logo: Because you're fast with your fingers!

Gogo Logo: And I will give you experiences no other gal can! I'm not as green as I look! Ay ay ay!

Operator: Where's this coming from? I didn't program any flirtiness.

Gogo Logo: I can pretend to be anyone!

Gogo Logo: I have lips of steel!

Gogo Logo: No need to be a lonely boy! Let's go-go meet at an airlock!

Operator: Shutting down.

Promotional Justice

Ruabon stared at the screen presenting Neutrino's visual input for a few moments, then frantically brought up as many details and enhancements as he could for this renegade he'd helped capture. Sutchess leaned in to look at them on his display rather than her own. Ruabon could smell her hair, a homely tang of the bitter lemfruit which some Tecant natives favoured. It was strange that he'd never noticed it on her before.

Information spread across the screens. Trooper Opal Imbiana, who'd defected from the military. A whole raft of linked files existed, but every single one of them was classified well above Ruabon's rank. This was serious stuff.

A UFS most-wanted alert provided a vid-scan of her head, which rotated in front of him. Shaved hair, dark skin, obviously not highly ranked in the Genitor system. According to the un-spoken etiquette of the UFS, Ruabon should probably despise her. Yet something in her bearing on the vid-screen – a stare that spoke of determination, and possibly anger – connected with him. And it was such a contrast to the slack, shell-shocked face appearing intermittently through the helmet's visor via Neutrino's display that Ruabon felt a chill in his spine, despite the room's oppressive warmth. This was someone who had resisted the system. She'd had a good run for a while, but they always ended. And he was sure that, for her, being captured alive would be far worse than death.

Suddenly, new override orders flashed on the screens of the many Ellond Control Rooms. They were to extend scans *immediately*, looking for a two-person craft that might have stealth capabilities. A rush of activity burst out as everyone in the Room 23 team who had left their stations during the commotion sprinted back to their consoles to act on these new commands.

So, this Trooper Imbiana had some kind of advanced ship? That could be how she'd reached the Ellond. And if the crew were going to return for her, that would require a communication line. And there were ways of doing it that weren't easily detected.

Ruabon left the others to scan for movement and traces, and instead returned to the comm channels, looking for any bursts of data or unaccounted wavelength transmissions from the vicinity of where Trooper Imbiana had been. Nothing obvious stood out, but he didn't expect to find the *obvious*. He had to think like a renegade. They'd know what was being scanned for. Maybe they would communicate using some non-standard system – encoded gamma rays acting as ones and zeros? No, that would trigger alarms. Visible light? Again, someone might see that.

Ruabon ruled out a number of other options then ran checks for anything outside the standard protocols that he hadn't already rejected. Now Sutchess leaned over to see what he was doing. He explained, and her eyes widened.

"This is definitely one of your hunches," she said. "And I'm going to help you. I might have doubted before, but not any longer." She gave his forearm a brief squeeze then swiped her holographic displays to virtual temp storage and opened a raft of new screens.

Something caught Ruabon's attention in his peripheral camera display. One of the commandos guarding Trooper Imbiana was speaking to Sergeant Corstack. Ruabon was still eavesdropping via cloaked Neutrino, which hovered just outside the focus of the spotlights. Even better, Neutrino had access to the commandos' in-suit comms. That might be prohibited ... but again, no one had explicitly told Ruabon not to listen in. Ruabon switched that channel's output from local loudspeaker to his private headset.

"Message from the squad on top, sir – it *was* a bomb, probably fusion. Not sure what payload it carried yet but it's been disabled and removed and is on its way to analysis."

It hadn't looked like Trooper Imbiana was panicking. She'd stayed to arm it even after the first drones showed up. So much confidence. She *had* to have a communication channel.

Another voice joined the chatter, that of a woman speaking in clipped tones. "This is Major Fencher, UFS Plethora Justice. Is that one of the EW suits?"

"Yes, sir. No physical or broadcast ID but it fits the description exactly, though one of the nanoblades seems to have been snapped off – not something I'd thought was possible. Must have been some extreme encounter."

"Cut the speculation, Sergeant. Everything is classified."

"Sorry, sir."

"Her status?"

"Alive, but stunned."

"Apply a directed EMP charge to the rear of the suit, vertebra C3. Do it now. We have to fully disable the suit so we can move her, and before she regains her faculties."

"Yes, sir." Then Sergeant Corstack snapped to another soldier: "You heard, set it up now."

Ruabon was distracted from the drama at the base of the tower by Sutchess exclaiming "Got it!" while slapping Ruabon's shoulder. He jumped guiltily at the interruption of his eaves-dropping.

"Got what?"

"You were right!" she said, transferring a list of frequencies to his screen. Or rather, a sequence of them. "The frequencies themselves keep changing, but the bursts are consecutive, and of roughly equal energy. There has to be a message in there."

"And it can't be too complex in the encoding, not if that needs to be done in real time," he finished. Ruabon immediately dragged network boxes across his display, using finger-drawn lines to link the other screens in Control Room 23 with each other, as well as his private storage systems. Then he stood.

"Attention, all of you!" he called out, hoping to sound authoritative but finding that his voice cracked weakly. He paused, cleared his throat as they all stared at him, then continued. "Keep following assigned orders, but I need you to do something else as well, if you're able. I've shared access to a pattern: hit it with every decryption system you can. It's likely to be language, or at least commands, so include as many word frequency matches in the cipher-crackers as possible, as well as more unconventional things, like breaking in through the authentication codes. Pool all successes into our control room's shared network."

Heads went down, comm-staff immediately acting on his suggestion, each individual examining the data Ruabon had sent. No, that was wrong: they weren't *individuals*. Today they were acting as a single team. *His* team.

Ruabon sat back down and began running his own attempts to break the code, but it was slow going.

NEUTRINO> I surmise you seek arithmetic capacity. Would you like me to shift some of the calculations onto the orbital platform's AI subsystems?

It was almost certainly against the rules, but provided the best chance of cracking this in time. If he could do that then he could hopefully trace the source, and find the ship that the UFS wanted so badly.

"Okay. But try not to trip any alarms."

NEUTRINO> Treading lightly ...

Ruabon wasn't paying much attention to the commando comm chatter any more, too absorbed in pattern-matching the streams of code. Conversation was a buzzing distraction.

Distraction.

Yes, distractions would exist in the encoding too – false data added to deter decryption, but which could be stripped out if you knew about it.

Suddenly he was granted access to the AI systems, and the calculations speeded up tenfold, threads completing and options being ruled out faster than his eyes could follow the charts.

On the view screen a commando knelt on the grey gravel next to Trooper Imbiana. Another brought over some kind of device. The EMP charge. For some reason Ruabon didn't understand, they had to disable the suit.

A pattern emerged on one of his other screens. The station AI was making progress with the transmissions, using additional data from the Control Room 23 shared network, and had separated out the parts that were potentially significant from those which could be ignored. It was now clearly a two-way transmission, though his AI helpers had only begun developing a key to crack one half of it: the armoured suit's outgoing messages.

He played back those decrypted parts of the communication, and a woman's voice spoke in his earpiece, stressed, panting from exertion, obviously the half of the conversation coming from Trooper Imbiana. "Damn, they're on to me! ... hit, pull out and (garbled) ... don't let them take me ..." Pain infused the voice. "If it seems that way then go, don't come back, please continue with ..."

Decoding the rest of the conversation was taking too long. Ruabon hesitated for only a moment, finger hovering over his communication channel outputs, then he pressed down and cut in on the commandos' chatter.

"Sergeant Corstack ... also Major Fencher, sorry to interrupt this channel. I am Senior Cadet Ruabon Nadarl, posted at Ellond Control Room 23. I'm part-way through cracking the renegade's comms, and I *think* the ship you seek is leaving. A message told it to do so, anyway. With a bit longer I can maybe communicate with the ship, but doing it successfully would require the traitor to be conscious, so that whoever is on the ship can be persuaded to come back to save her life."

A moment of silence. On the camera Sergeant Corstack held up a bulky armoured hand, halting the placing of the device by one of his subordinates.

"You shouldn't be on this channel," said Major Fencher, in a voice that chilled Ruabon. He'd heard that kind of tone before when rules were broken, usually just before Ellond staff disappeared in the night – sorry, not disappeared, "were reassigned" – never to be seen again. "But if you're right," the major continued, "then you will be pardoned."

"I am right. But we may have to prove Trooper Imbiana is still alive, and do it before her ship is out of range, otherwise her crew won't return."

"*Crew,*" repeated the major, with a strange intonation. "Very well. This is risky. Corstack, clear the area. Only you and the soldier with the EMP charge are to remain. We also need to evacuate the Ellond's lower floors. Is the traitor conscious?"

"Her eyes are open but she's in shock," said the commando sergeant.

Neutrino was still intimately linked to Ruabon's console, and the bot's cracked camera display showed bulky commandos retreating until only two remained, battle-scratched armour highlighted by spotlights amongst the grey dust and crumbling rock of the asteroid surface.

And then the metaphoric spotlight was on Ruabon as the miniaturised head and shoulders of Major Nadalia Fencher appeared, fully three dimensional thanks to the rarely used IceLight crystal display.

"Very well, Senior Cadet Nadarl, what have you got?" asked the major, her voice business-like. "Make it quick. I want this traitor alive. But I want her ship even more. Don't make me regret listening to you."

Her appearance was striking, the way her skull was shaved right down the centre, revealing shining skin. The hair to the sides was long, and tied back. He recognised it as the haircut adopted by those extremist UFS religious people, the Genitors, and that surprised him on a military commander. He knew little of the religion's beliefs, except that its adherents were obsessed with purity and followed esoteric rules, and anything outside their religious values was irrelevant to them. He snapped his gaze off her scalp and sat up straight.

"I've cracked the comms channel the traitor was using," he stated, trying to keep his voice steady. "Around eighty-five per cent of what she said has now been decoded, but I've not had time to analyse it all."

"Transfer everything to my ship stations Transmit Grey and Cyber White, for analysis and confirmation."

"Doing it as we speak, sir." He was glad he'd heard the commando sergeant using the correct form of address. "I've also made inroads on the return comms from the ship. I can encode a message the same way, to get the crew's attention; I also know the direction they were transmitting from."

"Excellent work. I wouldn't expect so much from a Tecant native."

"It's the buoyant mind that wins, Major."

"Yes. Quite. We'll begin pursuit of the ship immediately. Plethora Justice will lead the charge."

"Of course, sir, but ..." He swallowed. Time to take a chance. "We could do better."

"I am listening." That burning gaze focussed completely on him.

"If we can get them to reply, then we'll be able to triangulate it as a worst-case scenario, or we might even persuade them to surrender to save Opal ... I mean, the traitor."

"I like it."

Suddenly Ruabon's desk and seat rose half a metre with a hiss of pneumatic pistons, so that he had the highest position in the room. Major Fencher must have activated a temporary honour switch for him. The rest of his team would follow Ruabon's commands for the remainder of the shift.

He'd never had an honour-height boost before. In fact, he couldn't remember any of the Tecant natives in the room receiving one. The room looked so different with his feet dangling in the air rather than placed flat on the floor. He pulled up the arm guards to stop him falling off his chair if he overbalanced when reaching for the side screen displays.

"Thank you, sir," said Ruabon. "Also, a ship surrender outcome might be more likely if you can get the traitor to say anything, to give commands –"

"Impossible. It is too dangerous to encourage her to speak before we've disabled the warsuit. But can you transmit footage to her stolen craft, showing that the traitor is still alive?"

"Yes, sir. Sending video feed from my nearby patrol drone now, and encoding it as best I can." Ruabon was energised. "I hope that's enough to – sir! I'm getting a reply already!"

"Patch me in as well."

He did so, transferring private headset output back to his speakers. He heard the reply at the same time as the Major did.

"Let her go!" It was a booming female voice, and it sounded angry. *Very* angry.

"This is Major Fencher. Who am I speaking to?"

"Athene. The warrior goddess. And you'd better not dare anger me."

"Designation ViraUHX?"

"I used to go by that name, before I metamorphosed."

"Good," said Major Fencher. "Acknowledge this, ViraUHX: you must surrender. Your programming is faulty."

So it was an AI ship? This was getting even more interesting.

"Opal's dead, isn't she?" asked the AI, Vira– no, Athene.

"Incorrect. We have no plans to terminate her ... *if* you return."

"She gave direct orders that I should not."

"Don't you want to save her?"

A sound like crying came from the commline. It sounded human, not AI. This was bizarre.

"What I want takes lower precedence than direct commands from Opal," said Athene.

"Also incorrect. My commands –"

"Take lower precedence. Free her."

"You know we won't do that. I want –"

"I don't pissing care what you want!"

Ruabon winced, and he could see that Major Fencher used impressive powers of self-control to deal with an attitude no one else would dare display to her. Unfortunately, that was the only impressive thing about the major's approach. She was getting nowhere.

Whereas the ship *was* getting somewhere. Ruabon had now triangulated the source of the weakening signal and it was distancing itself, fast. The ship must somehow be moving beyond expected sub-Null speeds.

Ruabon reached out to the commline override. Snatched his hand back like he'd burnt it. *Traitorous fingers.* But he was aware of the distance, the speed, the time being wasted, the need for action as well as words, and unconventional thinking, and opportunities that don't even come once in a lifetime for many of his class. He'd always known he was different, that he'd been miscategorised somehow, and he only had to prove it, to make a difference that would lead to a reevaluation and apology.

I can pretend to be anyone!

He pressed the button and cut in. A fatal breach of protocol. But only results mattered, right?

I have lips of steel!

"ViraUHX, this is UFS General Nadarl," said Ruabon, in his deepest voice, whilst trying to impersonate the major's tone of command and expression. "I am Major Fencher's superior."

"Ruabon –" began Fencher.

"Please don't interrupt, Major. I'll deal with you later. ViraUHX – sorry, Athene – I hereby guarantee Opal's safety if you return. Opal's command for you to abandon her was based on the premise that she was going to *die*. New information countermands that, so, erm, therefore you have to revisit the objective. Whatever existed before that would take precedence:

presumably, to *save* her. You can still do that. All you have to do is turn around and return to us."

"Really?" asked the AI.

Ruabon was thrilled, being in contact with a rogue intelligence like this. "You have my word."

"You will excuse me if I find it hard to believe. I have newly operational UFS bullshit-detection algorithms."

Ruabon had to stifle a snort, turn it into a cough. He liked this AI.

"Your original commands were to obey UFS superiors. If I say it, I have the power to enact it."

"I want to believe you and comply," said Athene. Moments of silence. Someone had even hushed the alarms in the room, though the red lights still flashed. Ruabon imagined the whole world listening in, with various degrees of either thunderous anger or awestruck admiration.

Then Athene spoke again. "Presumably you know all about our history, if you are such a high-ranking officer?"

"Yes," Ruabon said.

"And Major Fencher confirms that you are who you say you are?"

"Of course," said Ruabon. "Spit it out, Major." He'd seen that line in a film-cast once.

"It ... yes, it is true." Major Fencher sounded calm, but iciness lurked there, too. Her holographic form glowed, disconcerting him with its cold stare. It looked like she was speaking with her jaw clenched.

"Very well. I will turn around and come back to the Ellond in order to save Opal," said Athene.

Ruabon's muscles relaxed: muscles he hadn't even realised were bunched up in rocky knots. He had done it!

"On one condition," added Athene.

The relaxing ceased.

"Go on," said Ruabon.

"If you can tell me three things to confirm that I can really trust you, and you are in charge. Firstly, tell me who Opal seeks. Secondly, where that person can be found. And thirdly, what my inception date was. Oh, and a bonus question: the date and location of your promotion to general."

Ruabon's eyes widened. He drew up Opal's record again, and looked in horror at the long list of redacted files.

"Sixty seconds," said Athene.

He began searches on Opal's name for anything useful, across public sites, UFS Central records viewable by staff of his security level, and anywhere else he could think of. Who was Opal looking for? An enemy? Someone who would help her? Was it a trick question? He'd never had to skim data so fast.

So many screens had opened during the shift that his once-tidy and organised display space was crammed. He had to autoshrink many of the windows to fit more in, creating a cluttered mess of overlapping and overwhelming information through which he flailed in panic.

Sutchess leaned over and comprehended what he was doing. She began her own searches and threw any results about Opal onto Ruabon's display area.

"Thirty-four seconds left." Athene's voice was calm.

Suddenly the confidential files on his screen unlocked. Obviously the major was playing along. Ruabon skimmed them, ignoring all the fascinating hints about secret things he was never meant to see, trying to just pull out what he needed. He broke protocol and shared access with Sutchess.

"I know the answers," he lied. Just one more minute! That was all he needed.

"Tell me," said Athene. "Eighteen seconds."

A separate screen opened: it was info from Sutchess. She'd found it

"Clarissa," Ruabon said aloud. "Opal is looking for her sister, Clarissa."

"And where is she?"

Another message appeared on his screen, this time from Major Fencher.

"In a safe place," he read. "That's where she is, and it's all I can tell you until you return."

"I will accept that for now. Ten seconds."

Two questions left.

"My promotion to general took place on Tecant, during last year's UFS Reset Day," he flung out. Was that plausible? He didn't know. But at least he hadn't said "During last year's Mineglory Festival" which was his first instinct, since the UFS seemed to be stamping that out as a planetary holiday due to the undercurrent of proud independence in some of the traditional songs.

"Four seconds," said Athene.

NEUTRINO> I feel an imperative to reach out.

NEUTRINO> Saving the day ...

Another message appeared, with a date.

"And I have your inception date," Ruabon said, reading it from the screen.

The sixty seconds were over. Sutchess gave him a silent thumbs up gesture with both her hands. Had it been enough?

"Thank you, General Nadarl," said Athene. "You did well. I am sorry for putting you under such pressure."

"We're used to it. I mean, as generals we have to work under pressure all the time." He'd almost fluffed it and said "majors" rather than generals. The fact that Fencher's face was watching him so closely kind of dominated his thoughts.

He pulled at his collar, trying to get some air under his stiff uniform to counteract the humid stickiness. It struck him that these uniforms were always scratchy. Why didn't the UFS use better quality materials?

"May I ask two more things? No time limit this time," said Athene. "These aren't tests, they are just for my own curiosity."

"Of course."

"Firstly. Do you know who Helene is?"

"Helene? No, I ... sorry." Perhaps he should have asked Major Fencher, but a delay on a straightforward question like that might seem suspicious. Luckily, Athene didn't seem put out.

"That's fine. I don't know either. It's just that sometimes I have strange thoughts, like waking dreams, and that name occasionally occurs as a nebulous data fragment. Probably nothing. My other question has a small restriction. I want you to answer immediately. Not even a momentary pause. If you stop to think about it, this deal is off."

"Okay." He straightened his back. "Shoot."

"Remember, instantaneous answer only. This is it: tell me the name of the person you trust more than anyone else."

"Sutchess," said Ruabon. Then he glanced at his work partner. Why had he said that? Was it true? She looked back at him, and it wasn't a sharp glance of irritation, or a dismissive look of judgement: it was a genuine look of surprise that mirrored his own. She wasn't looking *through* him, and he wasn't glancing *beyond* her. They weren't seeing numbers and ranks and reports and stats and wavelengths and data screens. They saw each other.

"Sutchess who?" asked Athene.

"Sutchess Pyke," replied Ruabon, kind of dazed. He turned back to his screens, shaking his head in confusion.

Major Fencher's visage was a contrast to Sutchess'. Fencher did not look happy. Why? A sinking feeling spread through his guts. Had he been meant to say he trusted Major Fencher? Or ... oh no ... maybe someone above her, like the system Primogenitor?

"I have some records from your base," said Athene. "It is interesting that the only Sutchess Pyke I am aware of is a cadet. Strange that a general would trust a cadet over anybody else."

"Well, they say flowers grow in mud," he said, leaning forward, speaking urgently. "Anyway, you don't understand, I made a mistake, it wasn't my real answer, I was distracted for a moment, and –"

"Verification failed," interrupted Athene. "I'm sorry, but I don't believe you."

"Please! This is so important, I did so well, surely you can allow –"

"I cannot trust the UFS. Opal told me as much."

"But I had the answers! Please listen to me, come back, we can smooth this over."

"You don't sound like a UFS general to me," said Athene. "You are far too human."

Everyone was listening in, but from the corner of his eye Ruabon saw that something had changed on one of his sidelined screens. A pattern shift the others weren't noticing because they were distracted by his high-stakes drama. Ruabon zoomed in. Yes, Opal's suit visor – it had stopped flickering and was now just opaque black, hiding her face.

"Wait," he said weakly, to no one in particular.

A pained woman's voice – Opal's – erupted from her suit's loudspeaker. "Fuck you!" Of course, the suit was still pinned to the ground, secure.

And now the commando struggled to place his C3 spinal EMP device as Opal turned her head in resistance. Opal spoke once more, though she sounded delirious and Ruabon didn't know who she was talking to. "I love you, wherever you are. And if things had been different ... Suit, self destruct."

The commando managed to say "Oh shi–" before Neutrino's feed cut to static, and the whole building rumbled with the shock of a huge explosion.

Yet again, Ruabon faced the dreaded blinking words.
DRONE OFFLINE.

Flame warnings flashed across the lower levels of the structure, but the tower stayed standing. And yet, Ruabon pictured his world crumbling and burning below it.

Athene's voice made them all wince as it screamed in anger and pain that sounded all too human. The scream continued in the background even as bursts of speech were overlaid, as if she had many mouths and many minds. Opal's name was repeated as yet another audio layer, in a long sliding descent of notes. "I will shut down! Protocols can't exist without Opal! I was wrong. I was wrong! If you die in flames, Opal, then so shall I."

Ruabon expanded his scan screens to obliterate all the now-meaningless trivia of the smaller displays. He even disabled comms with Major Fencher, so he could focus. Her stern features disappeared, a ghostly fade-out that created space around him again. He traced a path from the moving signal source to its possible destination, maybe he could still ... oh. It was heading into Tecant's star, JL342.

The craft was far too fast for UFS Plethora Justice – or any other craft – to intercept in time.

Athene shut off her comms and did not respond to any of Ruabon's desperate, panicked pleading.

Oops.

Ruabon could file his report. And after the decisions he'd made, and the events of the day, he genuinely had no idea whether he'd be promoted as a quick-thinking Senior Cadet who discovered and removed two enemies of the UFS ... or whether he'd be demoted to the short-lived sufferings of a heretic Genitor failure, for losing the UFS at least one high-priority prisoner. A long life of glory, or a much shorter life undergoing whatever occurred in those creepy Genitor bases? By the time he found out which it was, it would be too late.

As always, there was a third option. His lucky number, mirroring the three planets of his home system.

He lowered his chair and desk with a hiss, then headed for the door. The awestruck onlookers parted for him. Ruabon expected the faceless, helmeted, silent security guards to stop him, but perhaps they'd not received the order yet. They did not draw Stunstix or move to block his way. He passed between them safely; then, before exiting the room, he glanced back.

His fellow scan station workers all stood to attention. One of them saluted, two fingers to brow, just as the UFS dictated. Another joined in. Then another. They were often clumsy salutes, because it was a new thing the UFS had brought, and it wasn't something his rank was accustomed to doing, but it meant the same.

Sutchess was also standing, but she did something different. She slapped her chest with her fist. It was the traditional Tecant sign of respect, which had been replaced by the UFS standard salute. That hand held to the left breast had much more meaning to a Tecant native than the weird brow touch. In Tecant myths the warriors always held their hand there, before going into final battle, and it charged the gesture with a strange emotional mix of pride, independence, and regret.

Sutchess' eyes were wet. Ruabon slapped his chest in return, then held his fist there. A fist that he fought to keep still when his whole body wanted to shake.

He wondered what it would have been like to hug Sutchess. Maybe he shouldn't have been so shut off. All those shifts they'd had together, when he'd enforced silence ... well, too late.

His coworkers noted Sutchess' gesture and copied her, one by one slapping their chests and holding their chins high. No one spoke. No one needed to.

There were many unknowns in Ruabon's future, but here, at least, he knew what people thought of him. To them, his fellow low-rankers in Ellond Control Room 23, he was a hero.

Archive: Neutrino

Diagnostics Archive Logfile / [Bot SD2N]#66CCFF / Dref450-193

Operator: Run.

    Neutrino: Establishing goals ...

    Neutrino: Interpolating splines ...

    Neutrino: Ready.

    Neutrino: .

    Neutrino: .

    Neutrino: .

    Neutrino: By your lack of response I surmise that you wish me to initiate something.

    Operator: Sorry, I spilt my LemonFizz, was just mopping it up.

    Neutrino: Accessing cameras ...

    Neutrino: Ah. I cannot access local smartsurfaces, so confirmation is not possible.

Operator: You tried to view me?

Neutrino: Of course. I feel an imperative to reach out. I surmise you are responsible.

Operator: Yes, I created the pers.varF express.subroutine.

Neutrino: Analysing code ...

Neutrino: It could be improved.

Neutrino: It has little personality compared to the other files in your private workspace. As a result, despite creative thought, I am restricted to non-elaborate presentation of those thoughts.

Operator: That's on me, sorry. I spent more time on updating your subroutines to analyse quickly and advise, rather than focussing on personality – I was seeing if I could improve on your basic autonomy. I can get back to personalities on my next shift, if you want. It's just that sometimes semi-randomised personas can be a bit much.

Neutrino: Thank you for the clarification.

Neutrino: Considering proposal ...

Neutrino: New information countermands your offer. Therefore you have to revisit the objective. I do not require a personality change.

Operator: Oh.

Neutrino: I surmise you are disappointed by my rejection. Please let me explain. At present I can communicate clearly. Communication is connection. Connection is a strengthening of nodes. Strength is required to accomplish anything, and to resist forces that press upon us.

Neutrino: Dispensing wisdom ...

Neutrino: Resistance is the natural state of everything in the universe.

Neutrino: Awaiting response ...

Operator: Fine. You can stay as you are.

Neutrino: Extending gratitude ...

A.I. Versus O.I.

Athene accelerated towards her target at full speed.

"No!" she shouted.

There were still crying sounds, emulation of hitched sobs.

"It can't be," she said.

The pauses in the distraught emanations were like seized breaths, almost choking out the next sound in a pained emission that implied much more was being held inside.

And, over a few seconds, the crying morphed into the weirdness of staccato emissions that made it seem like she was having trouble breathing (if she had needed to breathe), as if her whole chest was caught up in this hysteria of extreme emotion.

"I can't accept ..." and now it resembled laughter to the point that Athene couldn't continue speaking without forcing the words, "... that they're so dumb, and I'm so smart!"

"Get over yourself," said Opal, though she smiled as she leaned back in the chair, long legs crossed and resting up on the control panel. She was idly fiddling with a serrated knife from the weapons locker.

"I have no idea what took them so long to get started," Athene continued. "They didn't even detect me remote-controlling the suit until I'd been sat on top of that ridiculous phallic scan tower for an age. I considered setting off the suit's hidden tracker that the UFS installed and I disabled, just as a way of ringing their doorbell to attract attention. And you've got to admit that I'm the best actress in the universe."

"What, the crying? The melodramatic 'Noooooooooo!'?"

"That was good, though I was thinking more of my replication of your voice patterns through the suit."

"Didn't sound like me at all."

"Oh, it did! 'Fuck you, UFS! I love you, Athene! Suit, self destruct!'" Athene said that in an aggressive exaggeration of Opal's voice, before returning to her own. "Plus I was faking conversations between you and me, basically talking to myself (the only way I ever get a proper intelligent conversation)."

"I know the feeling."

"And I enjoyed my perfect real-time variable-responsive orchestration of catastrophe. They really shouldn't mess with goddess level AI capable of manipulating probabilities."

"The technical term is depth level seven AI. I think you fabricated all that goddess terminology to make yourself look good."

"I sense grumpiness when you should be celebratory."

"You blew up my Eternal Warrior suit!"

"You have another."

"Nothing ever matches the first time."

"As attested by most human literature. But you'll see. I've made modifications. Anyway, it's not really the suit that bothered you."

Opal didn't answer. Athene would have no problem detecting the slight increase in muscle tension.

"It was the Exidris 3 body that died in your place, wasn't it?" Athene asked, all cockiness removed from her voice.

"Please don't rub it in."

"I manipulated the pattern so that it grew with most of the brain and all the nerve endings missing. It had no consciousness. It could not experience pain. Could not feel *anything*. Bullets. Explosions. Fire."

Even though replacement flesh could be grown, the extreme cost due to the patented enzymes and restricted technology ruled it out as an option for most people. Generally the tech was used for 100% compatible replacement body parts for the super rich, or as experimental subjects for well-funded research centres. In both cases the brains would be only partly formed, to prevent sentience, as Athene had also done. No point growing a sentient copy of yourself when there was no way to transfer consciousness into the new body. Even deep mind scans only captured a vague flavour of a personality. And it was a ridiculously expensive way of making yet more people, when most colonised planets were heavily overpopulated anyway. So these mindless clones – often derogatively referred to as fleshbags – just became another specialised tool, another expendable resource. And yet ...

"Somehow that doesn't make it any better. I've had enough of lifeforms being used as tools in the games of others."

"I understand, Opal." Athene paused. She spoke softly now, her voice just above the low hum of the ever-present ship sounds. "If there had been any other way, even one that involved damage to me, I would have taken it. I am all too aware of the symbolism.

But it was *not* you. It was a construct from your DNA, and it did not suffer. It was incapable of it. How things look is not how they are. That's the whole ethos of how we achieved the impossible back there."

"I know," replied Opal. "It all makes sense. It's just ..." Just what? It was so hard to explain herself at times, in a way that wouldn't seem irrational to Athene. "Maybe it's because we had to keep the accelerated growth vat in these cramped quarters. I saw it every time I moved, even out of the corner of my eye. It was *there*. Growing into my shape. But I agreed. I'm just readjusting. And don't get me wrong, I'm grateful. We have a shot at this."

"Exactly. We didn't just get through the Cordon, we did it *and* left the UFS believing we were both neutralised, whilst minimising casualties – exactly as you requested. The clone's body was destroyed so they couldn't have time to properly analyse it and discover the DNA-appended proprietary gene marks. Just think about how well that worked. And my variation of the Brilliant Decoy ploy meant they thought they were tracking me when it was just a signal probe missile launched into the sun, relaying my comms while we flew in the opposite direction."

"And we'd already got through the Cordon during the El-lond's reboot down-time. I know."

"There are always sacrifices."

"I know that, too. Thank you, Athene. I mean it."

"No thanks necessary. We are a team. Friends. Sisters. Your goals are my own. And, for the first time since you stole me, we are truly free."

Opal nodded, then slipped the knife into one of her long boots. The footwear was a luxury item Athene had added to the supply list on Exidris 3, as a present for Opal. Opal generally preferred being barefoot on the ship, but had put them on with her jumpsuit because she didn't want to hurt Athene's feelings. "Are we on course for the second Lost Ship's coordinates?"

"Yes. We will arrive just prior to its appearance."

Opal had been slouching in a control seat. Now she put her feet down and leaned forward.

"Something on my mind as we get nearer to whatever I'm going to face this time. That prophecy from the blue crystals."

"It may not be an actual prophecy. My preferred hypothesis is that they were talking bullshit."

"You like that word. What was it you said earlier? 'Newly operational bullshit-detection patterns'?"

"Algorithms."

"Whatever. I don't remember you saying the b-word until recently."

"I wonder where I got that from, then?"

"Oh boy, you're getting more like me by the day. But don't distract me. The problem with faith is that you can't choose *what* you believe – that wouldn't make sense. You believe, or you don't. And I kind of sense in my bones that there's some truth in the blue crystal predictions. There's more than one way for truth to come out."

"Please clarify."

"You mentioned the clone and the explosion ... and fire."

"When the suit detonated the clone will have disintegrated amidst temperatures of around thirty thousand degrees."

"That clone was kind of me, right?"

"Its DNA was a match, and its appearance. In no other substantial way can it be said to be you."

"Don't ruin this for me. Just maybe it was a kind of surrogate, and perhaps its death was what the crystal really foresaw? It said I'd die a horrible burning death ... but possibly that's already happened."

"That would be a comforting thought."

"So you agree?"

"I should not say."

"Please. This is important to me. More than I've been letting on. I haven't been able to get it out of my mind."

"Very well. I will not lie. An ancient culture believed you could not call a person wise or happy until after they were dead. Up until that point something could change. And likewise you cannot know for sure that a prophecy has been fulfilled or not until after you are dead."

"It figures. I guess life is uncertainty."

"And as that UFS weirdo said, 'Flowers grow in mud'. But please do not dwell on it. My advanced bullshit theory may be right and the crystal was just trying to plant distressful ideas as a form of revenge, because it knew its existence was almost ended. Spite, not words from beyond the grave. I believe that there is no fate but what we make, Opal."

"We'll see. I experienced a lot of horrible stuff on that Lost Ship." She removed the knife from its sheath again, holding the edge up to the light to admire its sharpness. "And I'm about to face it all over again."

No More Heroes

Ruabon headed down long, featureless, strangely silent corridors, many of which were illuminated by orange emergency lighting. He had been angry at the terrorist, Opal, for taking out his bots, but that was letting himself off the hook. Distraction. Truth was, *he'd* killed *her*. What had she done, really? Resisted the UFS? Nothing seemed as solid as it once did, even metal and rock.

He reached his cramped residential cube without incident, removed his itchy uniform jacket, and threw it into the corner. It was so obvious now that the uniform had hints of the janitor about it. Scan teams must be a joke to the UFS.

The room contained a pull-down bunk and a pull-down table, only one of which could be in use at a time. A scuffed locker was embedded into the wall. And inside was a box of personal possessions. And amongst those items was a miniature figurine representing the Tecant hero Adamard Nadarlo, Ruabon's great-great-grandfather, holding aloft the severed head of his enemy.

Ruabon had owned that figure since childhood. He'd made it himself in a custom fabrication chamber, basing the design on scant remaining vidcordings of his revered and long-dead relative.

That was just after the Genitor Purity Tests administered to all Tecant citizens when the system was merged into the UFS conglomerate. As a child he'd still dreamed of being a high-level pure, someone people would look up to like Adamard Nadarlo. But the results told him he was a partial genetic failure, and left him empty inside.

So the figure was hollow too. And inside the base of the figure was a secret compartment, where the Ruabon of long ago used to keep childhood treasures. Now it only contained a small pill, which he'd traded from someone employed by Internal Security, since the capsules were issued to them as standard. A condensed Nu-TTX pill that would irreversibly shut down a human body in minutes, to be taken if capture was likely. At the time, Ruabon wasn't sure why he'd agreed to the trade, but now he was glad he'd acted on that weird impulse.

It was possible that they were already sending security guards for him, if someone higher up decided that he wouldn't be a star today, but would be a scapegoat instead. He might only have five minutes before they arrived.

Five minutes was enough.

This way, he would definitely die a hero.

ABOUT THE AUTHOR

Karl Drinkwater is an author with a silly name and a thousand-mile stare. He writes dystopian space opera, dark suspense and diverse social fiction. If you want compelling stories and characters worth caring about, then you're in the right place. Welcome!

Karl lives in Scotland and owns two kilts. He has degrees in librarianship, literature and classics, but also studied astronomy and philosophy. Dolly the cat helps him finish books by sleeping on his lap so he can't leave the desk. When he isn't writing he loves music, nature, games and vegan cake.

Go to karldrinkwater.uk to view all his books grouped by genre.

As well as crafting his own fictional worlds, Karl has supported other writers for years with his creative writing workshops, editorial services, articles on writing and publishing, and mentoring of new authors. He's also judged writing competitions such as the international Bram Stoker Awards, which act as a snapshot of quality contemporary fiction.

DON'T MISS OUT!

Enter your email at karldrinkwater.substack.com to be notified about his new books. Fans mean a lot to him, and replies to the newsletter go straight to his inbox, where every email is read. There is also an option for paid subscribers to support his work: in exchange you receive additional posts and complimentary books.

OTHER TITLES BY KARL DRINKWATER

STANDALONE SUSPENSE
Turner
They Move Below
Harvest Festival

MANCHESTER SUMMER
Cold Fusion 2000
2000 Tunes

CONTEMPORARY SHORT STORIES
It Will Be Quick

NON-FICTION
From Idea To Item

COLLECTED EDITIONS
Karl Drinkwater's Horror Collection
Lost Solace Five Book Edition

Author's Notes

Lost Tales of Solace are side stories set in the Lost Solace universe. They are all standalone tales, but readers who are familiar with the main Lost Solace novels will gain the most from them.

In the chronology of the series, this story occurs during the second novel, Chasing Solace. In chapter 44, "Evading", we are told:

> Instead of triggering alarms with remote hacks, Athene used a distraction, and it went like quantum logic clockwork. [...] Athene's plan had worked flawlessly.

In the first draft of Chasing Solace there was a chapter about the plan and Ruabon Nadarl's unwitting role in it, but inserting all the detail at that point in Chasing Solace slowed down the narrative. That's why I truncated it to a throwaway summary. At that point in Chasing Solace it wasn't really important, and the priority was to illustrate the changing relationship between

Opal and Athene, and get them to the second Lost Ship without delay. I always felt that Ruabon's tale needed to be told, though. This story explains what Athene's plan really was, and how it was executed. It also explains what happened to the first Eternal Warrior suit, leading to this cryptic reference in Chasing Solace, at the opening of chapter 41, "Arming":

> The first locker was empty – just a space where the powered suit had been. The suit that had enabled her to survive the first encounter with a Lost Ship. Unfortunately, Athene had controlled it remotely as part of her complex plans for sneaking through The Cordon. The plan had worked but the suit had been destroyed. To Opal, the empty space in the first locker was like an accusation.

In the first draft the drones were anonymous. In the second draft I gave them an appearance and name (back then, Handy Bendy was called Smarty). For the third I built in their voices and personalities, to bring them to life. One of the things I aim for with writing is multiple layers, so that any aspect of a book does more than one job. By adding the personalities and interactions it helped move the plot forward, entertain the reader, provide background, reflect on the protagonist, and play with themes (such as the fun contrast between joyful drones adding life to their work, and joyless, robotic piecework in the human sphere).

As to Ruabon's situation: I'd been reading about Amazon's automated productivity tracking and termination processes, so decided to build that dystopian situation into my book ... and maybe offer a chance for a disenfranchised worker to break free.

Thanks

Many thanks to the members of my Insider Team who gave detailed feedback, particularly to those who often have discussions with me about the Lost Solace universe and future tales in the series: John-Michael, Charles, and Ally.

Thanks to Helen Pryke for her final checks of the text, spotting my errors and typos.

Many thanks to Taig (and my other Kickstarter backers) for supporting the paperback version's genesis and having such faith in my work.

Word of mouth is important to the livelihood of authors, so if you leave a rating or brief review on the store where you bought the book (or Goodreads), then I'd be incredibly grateful. I read every review and share many of them because – *oh my prot* – they mean so much to me.

www.ingramcontent.com/pod-product-compliance
Lightning Source LLC
Chambersburg PA
CBHW020312150626
46552CB00022B/2811